Little Phantom

Written by
Jill Atkins

Illustrated by
Heike Jane Zimmermann

One day, Little Phantom flew out of a crack in a yew tree.

"What do phantoms do?" she said.

"They frighten people," boomed Big Phantom.

"Oh good," said Little Phantom. "That will be fun! I will frighten some people now."

The west wind blew Little Phantom to the coast.

She saw some dolphins and a shark.

Then she spotted a ship.

"I will frighten the crew of that ship," she said to herself.

She swooped down to a man standing on the deck.

"Boo!" she said.

The man jumped!

"This is fun," said Little Phantom, as she left the crew and flew back to land.

Soon, Little Phantom spotted a girl sitting on a toy dog.

She flew down and floated next to the girl.

"Boo!" she said.

The girl clung to the dog.

Next, she saw a boy cooking a stew.

"Boo!" said Little Phantom.

The boy dropped his spoon in the stew.

Little Phantom grinned. "It's fun to frighten people," she said.

Then she flew down to a big park.

Lots of people were playing golf.

Just as a girl swung her club, Little Phantom flew near her.

"Boo!" she said.

The club missed its target.

Little Phantom was thrilled.

Next, she flew into a bedroom.

But what was that? There was an odd-looking thing in the corner.

"I'll frighten that thing," she said. "Boo!"

"Boo!"

"Oh!" said Little Phantom.

The thing had said "Boo!" back to her!

Little Phantom flew under the bed. She fluttered like the wings of a bird. That thing had frightened her.

Then there was a loud, deep sound.

"Little Phantom?"

It was Big Phantom.

Little Phantom floated out from under the bed.

"I was frightened," she said.

"What frightened you?" boomed Big Phantom.

Little Phantom pointed at the thing. Big Phantom threw back his arms and boomed.

"Oh, what fun!" he said. "Come and look."

Little Phantom floated near the thing.

She looked and looked. Then she grinned.

"Phew!" she said. "It's just me! I frightened myself!"